Leela's Tree

WITHDRAWN

Written by Claire Llewellyn

Illustrated by Priscilla Lamont

WITHDRAWN

KILKENNY COUNTY LIBRARY

D0277998

Leela has a tree.

The tree has flowers.

The tree has apples.

The tree has a swing.

The tree!

KK331055

KILKENNY COUNTY LIBRARY

Leela has a new tree.

Leela has the old tree, too.